Glamour! Talent! Stardom! Fame and fortune could be one step away for the kids of Fame School! All the students at Rockley Park, a school for the pop culture performing arts, are talented, but they still have to work hard. They must keep up their grades, learn about the professional side of the music business, improve their talent, *and* get along with their classmates. Being a star—and a kid—isn't easy. Things don't always go as planned, but one thing's certain—this group of friends will do their best to sing, dance, and jam their way to the top!

"We're going to be on TV!"

Lolly and Chloe linked arms as they made their way back to the dormitory through the cold, foggy night. It was very dark outside, and the lights marking the gravel path were blurred with mist. But once they were indoors, with Chloe's new lamp switched on and the curtains drawn, they soon began to feel warm and cozy.

"Imagine having a TV show all to yourselves," Chloe said, pushing bundles of underclothes into her dresser. "Wow!"

"I'm afraid Pop is going to go on and on about it, though." Lolly frowned. "She doesn't mean to be bigheaded, but if she's not careful, everyone will think that's exactly what she is."

Before Chloe could answer, the door opened. Pop burst in and flung her coat on her bed with a flourish. The peace in the room was shattered.

"Take one," she called, giggling, pretending to hold a camera up to her face. "Action! Lolly unpacks and chats with one of her biggest fans!"

"See what I mean?" said Lolly.

FAME SCHOOL
Secret Ambition

CINDY JEFFERIES

PUFFIN BOOKS

Thanks to Fran, the horse whisperer.

For my son Gavin, with much love.

PUFFIN BOOKS
Published by the Penguin Group
Penguin Young Readers Group,
345 Hudson Street, New York, New York 10014, U.S.A.
Penguin Group (Canada), 90 Eglinton Avenue East, Suite 700, Toronto, Ontario,
Canada M4P 2Y3 (a division of Pearson Penguin Canada Inc.)
Penguin Books Ltd, 80 Strand, London WC2R 0RL, England
Penguin Ireland, 25 St Stephen's Green, Dublin 2, Ireland
(a division of Penguin Books Ltd)
Penguin Group (Australia), 250 Camberwell Road, Camberwell, Victoria 3124, Australia
(a division of Pearson Australia Group Pty Ltd)
Penguin Books India Pvt Ltd, 11 Community Centre, Panchsheel Park,
New Delhi - 110 017, India
Penguin Group (NZ), 67 Apollo Drive, Mairangi Bay, Auckland 1311,
New Zealand (a division of Pearson New Zealand Ltd)
Penguin Books (South Africa) (Pty) Ltd, 24 Sturdee Avenue, Rosebank,
Johannesburg 2196, South Africa

Registered Offices: Penguin Books Ltd, 80 Strand, London WC2R 0RL, England

First published in Great Britain by Usborne Publishing Ltd., 2005
Published by Puffin Books, a division of Penguin Young Readers Group, 2007

1 3 5 7 9 10 8 6 4 2

Copyright © Cindy Jefferies, 2005
All rights reserved
CIP Data is available.

Puffin Books ISBN 978-0-14-240814-8

Printed in the United States of America

1. What's Wrong?

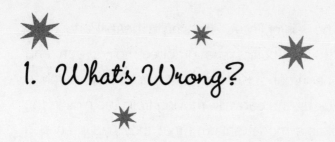

Poppy and Polly, the famous Lowther twins known as Pop 'n' Lolly, strutted along the catwalk behind the supermodel Tikki Deacon. All three were wearing exotic, designer dresses, with long, jewel-colored chiffon scarves. The music accompanying them roared out in a deafening blast that seemed to push them along, pace for pace in time with the music.

As Tikki reached the end of the walk, she turned abruptly and sashayed past the twins, the silk of her dress flowing around her ankles like rippling water. Pop turned, too, but something was wrong with her identical twin. Lolly had stopped, and was staring blindly into the lights as if transfixed. Pop turned again toward her sister, never missing a beat. Perfectly in time with the music, she grabbed Lolly's arm and yanked her around. Keeping a firm hold, Pop marched Lolly back up the catwalk, moving from the hips in the unmistakable model shimmy that they had practiced so much. Amused laughter and then loud applause saw them through the curtain to backstage.

"What on *earth* do you think you were doing?" demanded Tikki, glaring at them angrily. Tikki Deacon was almost as famous for her quick temper as she was for her fabulous looks and jet-setting lifestyle. "How dare you try to upstage me like that," she said. "You were supposed to turn and come straight off, not dawdle at the end like a couple of idiots! Who do you think you are?"

"Sorry," said Pop. "I think maybe Lolly's coming down with the flu or something."

"Well, keep her away from me, then!" Tikki snapped, backing into a rack of dresses. "I'm doing a fashion shoot in Acapulco on Tuesday and I don't want to miss it."

Lolly had begun to get changed where she stood. Backstage was chaotic, with hardly room to move. And someone had pushed a rack of clothes into the tiny corner that was supposed to have been reserved for the twins. There were models everywhere, and dressers scrambling to take the precious clothes as soon as they had been discarded. The chaos didn't worry Tikki Deacon, though. She pushed her way haughtily toward the door while Pop scowled at Lolly and flung off her own gorgeous dress in a fury.

"You nearly ruined *everything*," she hissed. "If we're not careful, Tikki will refuse to work with us again, and the designer won't have us back." She threw the dress and scarf into the arms of a waiting dresser and burrowed through the crush in search of her own clothes. In a few minutes she was back, wearing her jeans and jacket. "What's the matter with you?" she demanded, handing Lolly her jeans. "You're not usually such a dreamer."

"Sorry," said Lolly. "I'm not really coming down with the flu, though."

"I know *that*," said Pop disgustedly. "The flu was just the first excuse I could think of."

The girls made their way to the foyer of the hotel, where their mother was waiting for them, along with their agent, Satin Fountain-Blowers.

"Wonderful as always, my darlings," said their mom. She went to kiss them and then pulled away. "I wish you'd take that makeup off, though."

"We'll do it later," said Pop. "Can we go straight home?"

Satin nodded. "The taxi's waiting," she told them. "I know you're in a hurry to get to school for the beginning of the new term. Are you all right?" she added. Satin was very quick to pick up on their moods. She had been the twins' agent for years, ever since Pop and Lolly were really little and their mother had sent a photograph of them to Satin's agency. Satin had found the twins lots of modeling jobs, but today had been special, even for the famous twins. Working with the supermodel Tikki Deacon was a fantastic chance to raise their profile even higher, but any problems would reflect badly on Satin as well as the twins.

Pop yanked the remaining pins out of her hair. She shook it back over her shoulders and shot a tight smile at Satin.

"Of course we're all right," she said lightly. "Come on, Mom. Let's go. We've got to pack for school."

Pop was still annoyed with Lolly, and once they were in the taxi, she let her feelings show. "Did you see what happened, Mom?" she demanded as the taxi pulled away.

"What, darling?" asked their mother.

"Lolly! Missing her cue. I had to practically drag her off the catwalk! I was so embarrassed. And Tikki Deacon was furious. She thought we were trying to upstage her."

"Not at all," Mrs. Lowther protested mildly. "I thought it went very well. You both looked lovely as usual."

Pop slumped back into her seat, scowling furiously. "That's what you always say," she complained. Lolly said nothing.

"Well, you *do* both look lovely," their mother insisted. "Though you don't do your looks any favors when you glare at me like that."

Pop transferred her scowl to Lolly and their mother sighed. "You're so fiery," she told Pop. "Why can't you be more easygoing, like your sister? I wish you wouldn't get so worked up about little things, dear."

"It wasn't a little thing," Pop muttered. She folded her arms and stared out of the window without speaking until they reached home.

As soon as the twins were alone in their room, Pop raised the subject again.

"What's the matter with you?" she demanded. "You've done enough modeling not to freeze on the catwalk, even if we were with Tikki Deacon."

"It wasn't that," said Lolly, cleaning the makeup off her face. "I didn't have stage fright."

"Well, what *was* it, then?" Pop asked. "You know how hard Satin worked to get us that job. If the designer likes us, we could be modeling in *Paris* next year, but you almost wrecked everything."

Lolly finished cleansing her face and got up. Then she paused for a moment.

"It's just …"

"What?"

She shrugged wearily. "Oh, I don't know."

Pop looked at her sister. It was like looking into a mirror. Lolly had the same long, dark hair, styled in the same way, same wonderful coffee-colored complexion, same gorgeous dark eyes that everyone swooned over. Almost everything was the same. That was the way they'd made their name, by being a double dose of the same, flawless beauty. And they were so close that Pop usually knew exactly what Lolly was thinking, too. But at the moment, Lolly's thoughts were unreadable.

"Well, I'm sure *I* don't know if *you* don't," Pop said irritably. "But you made me feel like a real idiot today. We were perfect in rehearsal, and then, when it mattered, you missed the last turn. People were *laughing*."

"Sorry."

But Pop wasn't going to let her sister off with a brief apology.

"I hope you're not going to be scatterbrained when we're back at school," she warned.

Lolly gave her sister a withering look. Then she dragged her school trunk out into the middle of the room so she could start packing.

Pop sighed. If it hadn't been for Lolly messing up, today would've been perfect. Even going back for a new term at boarding school was something to look forward to.

Rockley Park School was an amazing place. It was the best talent school in the country for aspiring pop singers, musicians, and technicians. It taught them everything they needed to know about making it in the music industry. So as soon as Pop had mentioned that she'd always dreamed of being a pop singer, Satin had recommended the school. And it was absolutely everything she had promised them it would be.

"Just because you're successful models at the moment," Satin had said, "it doesn't mean that you will be forever. You need something else as well, and pop singing is a brilliant idea!"

Both Pop and Lolly had good voices, great stage presence, and were already well known, so they were almost halfway to being pop stars already. They'd made some good friends at Rockley Park, and were very happy there, but it was a competitive business, and Pop and Lolly couldn't afford to be complacent.

"You *aren't* going to mess up at school, are you?" insisted Pop.

"Look. I lost it for a moment, that's all," said Lolly. "Stop picking on me, okay? I mean it." She rummaged under her bed and came out with a scruffy pair of sneakers, which she shoved into a plastic bag.

Pop sighed again. "Okay," she agreed reluctantly before opening the lid of her own trunk.

It was very unsettling for Pop that she still didn't know what Lolly had been thinking when she missed her cue. They were both too professional to lose concentration easily. But Pop knew that the subject was now closed. Lolly was by far the more easygoing of the twins, but even *she* could dig her heels in sometimes. If Pop kept nagging her, they would end up having a really serious argument, and Pop didn't want that just before they went back to school. She glanced over at her sister. Lolly was methodically filling her trunk from the pile of clothes she'd sorted out that morning. Perhaps it was all right. Maybe her ditzy moment *was* a fluke, and wouldn't happen again.

Lolly was closing her trunk now. She snapped it shut and smiled at Pop, willing to be friends again.

"I can't wait to see Chloe and Danny and everyone else at school," she said. "I've even missed Tara! Come on, slowpoke. Get that trunk packed, Pop, and wipe off your makeup. Then we can tell Mom we're ready to leave. We haven't got much time, and we don't want to be late!"

2. Back at School

Pop and Lolly shared a bedroom at Rockley Park with two other girls, Chloe Tompkins and Tara Fitzgerald. Lolly loved her twin sister dearly, but it would be great to see Chloe again. They'd only met last term, but Lolly felt as if she'd known Chloe for years. Chloe was quiet and determined like Lolly, and was a great antidote to Pop's high spirits.

As soon as their parents had dropped them at school, the twins went up to their room in Paddock House. Judging by the luggage already there, Chloe and Tara had arrived before them. They were probably in the dining room.

"Come on," Lolly urged her sister. "Let's go to the dining hall and say hello to everyone."

"Okay."

On their way out of the dormitory, Lolly paused to look in their mailbox.

"We've got a note!" she said in surprise. She opened it and Pop read it over her shoulder.

"What can Mrs. Sharkey want?" Pop asked.

Lolly shrugged.

"Goodness knows," she replied. "We haven't been here two minutes and already the principal wants to see us. I hope there's nothing wrong."

They went straight over to the main house, where Mrs. Sharkey had her office on the second floor. But on the way past the dining room, Lolly spotted Chloe, Danny, and Tara waiting in line for their dinner.

"Hey, Chloe!" Lolly rushed over and hugged her friend happily. "Did you have a good Christmas? It's great to see you!"

Pop threw her arms enthusiastically around Danny.

"Whoa!" Danny said, disentangling himself good-naturedly. "Don't knock me over!"

"I had a fantastic time, thanks," said Chloe. "But it's good to be back. Hi, Pop. Happy New Year!"

"Hi!" Pop gave Chloe an enormous hug, too.

"Ready to rock-and-roll?" said Chloe with a giggle. "I can't wait for my first singing lesson now that I've got my voice back at last."

Chloe had a huge singing voice, but had needed lots of help to get it together last term. It was great to see her so happy now.

"Let's grab a table," suggested Tara, picking up her tray impatiently.

"We can't," said Lolly, looking anxious. "We got a message to go and see the principal. But we just had to say hello first."

"Well, you couldn't have done anything bad yet, could you?" joked Danny. "You've only just arrived!"

"That's true," agreed Lolly. "Come on, Pop...we might as well get it over with."

"See you back here," Pop called as they made their way to Mrs. Sharkey's office. "Wish us luck!"

It wasn't long before the twins returned. Pop was looking very pleased with herself, though Lolly's expression was harder to read.

Chloe had saved them some chocolate cake. Everyone knew that Rockley Park chocolate cake was Lolly's absolute favorite. She always had room for some, though at the moment she didn't seem to have much of an appetite. She turned the cake into crumbs with her fork and pushed them around her plate, while Pop sat grinning at everyone.

"What did Mrs. Sharkey want?" asked Chloe.

"She's going to make you wear name tags so the teachers know which of you is which," Tara suggested.

Lolly shook her head. "No," she said, biting her lip. "It's not that."

Pop's eyes met Chloe's and her whole face dissolved into a huge grin again.

"We're going to be on TV!" Pop burst out, and then blushed furiously. She gulped a huge swig of juice and, after swallowing the wrong way, started coughing and spluttering. Chloe thumped her on the back, and Tara passed a napkin over so Pop could dry her watering eyes.

"It's that show *Kids in the News*," said Lolly, while Pop was still recovering. "Apparently, they want to do a piece on us trying to break into the music industry, as well as having a career in modeling."

"Not a *piece*," Pop corrected her sister hoarsely. "A whole *show*! And they want to film it here, at the school! It'll be fantastic!"

"Oh, great." Tara sighed irritably, pushing her plate to one side. "There'll be no shutting them up now. Life will be impossible."

Lolly looked at her sympathetically. Tara wasn't the easiest of people to get along with, but Lolly had the uncomfortable feeling that Pop might rattle on about this television show until everyone was completely sick of it—and of them.

"I think it's great," said Danny. "They might want to film you singing, and maybe," he continued with a hopeful smile, "you might want a drummer."

"Or a *dancer*!" added Marmalade Stamp, one of Danny's roommates, who had just joined them.

Chloe laughed. "If we all have our way, there won't be any room for you two," she said to Pop and Lolly. "The show will be full of us, trying to get noticed!"

"I expect we'll only be on for a couple of seconds," Lolly warned them.

"No!" Pop protested. "Don't be silly. It's a *whole show*! Thirty minutes about *us*! What an opportunity!"

"She's right," Chloe told Lolly. "You never know what might happen after you're on TV!"

"True." Lolly pushed her chair back and stood up. "Well, I'm going to get unpacked," she said. "Anyone else coming?"

"I will," said Chloe. "I won't feel settled in until I've got all my stuff organized."

Lolly and Chloe linked arms as they made their way back to the dormitory through the cold, foggy night. It was very dark outside, and the lights marking the gravel path were blurred with mist. But once they were indoors, with Chloe's new lamp switched on and the curtains drawn, they soon began to feel warm and cozy. Chloe put the CD she'd gotten for Christmas in her player and Lolly made up her bed with a new duvet cover she'd brought from home.

"Imagine having a TV show all to yourselves," Chloe said, pushing bundles of underclothes into her dresser. "Wow!"

Back at School

"I'm afraid Pop is going to go on and on about it, though." Lolly frowned. "She doesn't mean to be big-headed, but if she's not careful, everyone will think that's exactly what she is."

Before Chloe could answer, the door opened. Pop burst in and flung her coat on her bed with a flourish. The peace in the room was shattered.

"Take one," she called, giggling, pretending to hold a camera up to her face. "Action! Lolly unpacks and chats with one of her biggest fans!"

"See what I mean?" said Lolly.

3. A Go-Between

In spite of Pop and Lolly's exciting news, school life had to start as usual the next morning. Rockley Park might be a school for budding singers and musicians, but the students still had to study all the usual school subjects. Lolly had always found the academic work easy, and really enjoyed most of her classes, but Pop struggled through a morning of math, English, and history before she and Lolly had their first private singing lesson with Mr. Player.

"Mrs. Sharkey has told me all about *Kids in the News*," he said in a pleased voice. "What a great start to the term! They may want to film you during one of our lessons, and possibly even singing a whole song.

I'll give some thought as to what you could perform."

After they'd warmed up their voices, Pop found it difficult to concentrate, so Mr. Player sent her to pour some water for herself and Lolly.

"I know you're excited," he said. "But you need to concentrate, Pop. Have a sip of water and calm down. Look at Lolly. She's managing to stay focused."

"She's *always* calm," grumbled Pop. But she did her best to put *Kids in the News* out of her mind and think more about the lesson.

"You go out of tune when you stop concentrating, so let's hear you sing these notes as perfectly as you can," Mr. Player told them both. Mrs. Jones played the notes on the piano and Pop listened hard.

"Much better," Mr. Player praised the twins when they'd finished. "And on your own, Pop. Yes. *Now* you're thinking about what you're doing. Well done."

After the long lunch break, when lots of students had individual lessons, there was an art class. This was a subject Pop really liked.

"Come on, Danny!" She giggled, leaning over to

look at his work. "You'd never get on *Kids in the News* as an artist! What's it supposed to be?"

Danny was doing his best, but he'd never been very good at drawing. He looked rather embarrassed, and Lolly came to his rescue.

"Don't tease him," she said. "You wouldn't think it was so funny if Danny laughed at you in chemistry. And stop going on about *Kids in the News*. I'm getting sick of it."

Pop stared at her sister. "This could be our big break," she told Lolly. "And you're *sick* of it?"

"Come on now, girls, stop talking and concentrate," said the art teacher, and Pop had to drop the subject.

By dinnertime everyone was ready for a break, but although normal lessons were over, the school day hadn't finished. There were still extra music lessons, practice to fit in, and later on, homework to do.

Pop couldn't help talking about *Kids in the News* again as she and Lolly went in to dinner.

"Do you think the television crew will just follow us around all day, or give us the chance to perform?" she asked.

Lolly put her tray back on the pile with a clatter.

Pop looked surprised. "What?" she said. "What's the matter?"

Lolly looked away. "I'm not hungry," she muttered. "I'm going for a walk."

"Oh! I'll come with you, then," Pop offered. "We can always have dinner a bit later."

"No," Lolly told her firmly. "I want to go on my *own*."

Before Pop could reply, Lolly had turned on her heel and left the dining room. Pop stared after her, and was still loitering uncertainly by the dinner trays when Chloe came in.

"Where is everyone?" asked Chloe, dropping her bag on the floor.

"Danny's got a drum lesson," said Pop. "I think Marmalade's in the dance studio, and I don't know about Tara."

"What about Lolly?" asked Chloe.

"Oh, she's gone off on a walk ..." Pop said resentfully.

"Oh?"

"She *never* goes for walks without *me*," said Pop

25

miserably. "I don't know what's up with her. She's been in a strange mood ever since the fashion show we did with Tikki Deacon, and I can't figure it out." The more Pop thought about it, the more upset she felt about her twin's behavior. At the fashion show, Pop had been annoyed, a few minutes ago she'd felt bewildered, but now she was starting to feel a little sad. She hadn't ever felt lonely and abandoned by her twin before, but she did now, and they were horrible feelings to have.

"I'm beginning to think she doesn't want to be a *twin* anymore," Pop told Chloe, feeling very sorry for herself. Two huge tears plopped onto her plate and she rubbed her eyes.

"No!" Chloe protested. "I'm sure she doesn't feel like that. You both seemed fine earlier."

"I thought so," Pop agreed, sniffing. "We were coming in for dinner, and everything was okay, but then Lolly said she was going to go for a walk instead. I said I'd go, too, but she told me she wanted to be alone!"

"Well, that's not so bad," Chloe said. "Everyone needs to be alone *sometimes*."

"But the only time we split up is when we've had an argument!" Pop insisted. "And we haven't! So why does she suddenly hate me?"

"I'm sure she *doesn't* hate you," said Chloe. "I imagine hating your twin would be like hating yourself! Perhaps it's her hormones. My mom says hormones can make you really grouchy when you're our age."

"You could be right," Pop admitted. "But I don't think so. She just didn't want me hanging around, and I don't know why. We've always known what each other is thinking, but now I don't and it's horrible." Pop clutched her friend's arm. "*You* ask her what's wrong, Chloe. She'll tell you."

Chloe frowned. "I don't know. She might think I was interfering."

Pop shook her head. "I'm sure she wouldn't. Please!"

Chloe sighed. "All right. I'll try to talk to her."

"Go now!" Pop said. "I bet she's talking to those horses in the corral, telling them stuff she won't tell me." Just saying it made Pop half believe it, and another couple of tears rolled down her cheeks.

"Okay!" Chloe told her. "I'm going. Don't cry." She put her jacket back on and picked up her bag. "I'm sure it can't be as bad as all that!"

Chloe headed over to the corral, which was opposite their dorm. Sure enough, there was Lolly, hanging over the corral rails, stroking one of the horses on his neck.

"Hi!" Lolly smiled at Chloe, her breath coming in puffs of vapor in the cold air.

"Don't you want any dinner?" Chloe asked awkwardly.

Lolly stopped stroking and shook her head. "Not really. I had an enormous lunch, and I wanted to get outside for a while instead."

"Oh." Chloe hesitated. "I just wondered what you were up to. Pop was having dinner by herself and I thought..." She trailed off and Lolly groaned.

"Pop asked you to come and find me, didn't she?"

"Not find, *exactly*," said Chloe, looking rather embarrassed.

"Is she upset?" Lolly asked.

"A little," Chloe told her.

Lolly sighed. "I just needed some space, that's all. Pop can be so…well, you know what she's like. And I wish she wouldn't keep going on about that TV thing. It's really getting to me."

"But why?" asked Chloe. "I mean, it *is* exciting. I'd be thrilled if it were me doing it. Don't you think it could be wonderful for your career?"

Lolly looked at her friend. Chloe was doing her best to be helpful, but Lolly's secret thoughts were a million miles away from what Chloe and Pop were getting excited about. It seemed that everyone else was pleased about the TV show, so why couldn't she feel the same? But Lolly *couldn't* feel the same, however hard she tried. In fact, the more it was mentioned, the less she wanted anything to do with being interviewed for television.

"Is something wrong?" Chloe asked. "It's just that Pop was upset, and now you seem miserable too."

"Not really," Lolly answered, trying to push her gloomy thoughts away. "I think it's just that Pop is so enthusiastic and up for everything, and sometimes I'd rather be quiet. That's always been the biggest difference between us. Usually, it doesn't matter," she added. "I just let her get on with it and tag along. But sometimes I'd like to be a person by myself, not half of Pop 'n' Lolly. Do you understand?"

Chloe nodded. "I feel that way with my little brother sometimes," she said, "when he won't leave me alone. But he's not at school with me. It must be much harder when you're a twin because you do *everything* together. Now Pop is scared you don't like her. I know she gets upset easily, but she said that maybe you don't want to be her twin anymore!"

Lolly sighed again and her breath misted in the cold air. "That's stupid. Pop always goes over the top about everything. Of *course* I still want to be her twin, *and* she knows it. Believe me, the last thing I want to do is upset her."

"Sorry," Chloe said. "I didn't mean to interfere."

"You're not interfering," Lolly said, determined to cheer up. "It's great to have you for a friend because you really care." She reached over the fence and gave the horse a last pat. "Come on, Chloe. Let's go in. It's freezing! I wouldn't mind a drink, and if Pop's still at dinner, I can give her a hug and tell her not to be so stupid. She's got to learn that I like my own company sometimes. It's just silly to want to do *everything* together!"

4. Good News

The next morning was the first dance class of the term. All the students had to take two dance classes each week to help them keep fit, even if they weren't interested in dancing as a career. It helped everyone with rhythm and coordination, and it was fun, too.

"Let's do some stretching to warm up first," said Mr. Penardos, the dance teacher, in his lovely Cuban accent. "Arms ou' to the side, and . . . stretch up. On one leg, hold the ankle. Feel that stretch. Now the other leg. Good!" He put on a heavy disco beat and clapped his hands.

"Follow me, ev'r'body! Walking forward, two, three, four, and . . . back, two, three, four. Jump, jump, three, four, ver' nice, Marmalade!"

Danny rested his hands on his knees to catch his breath as soon as they stopped. "I'd forgotten how tough this was," he said to Lolly, panting hard. "It's all right for Marmalade, he's going to be a professional dancer, but I don't use my muscles like this for drumming!"

"Have you decided if you want any dancers for your TV show?" asked Marmalade, who was hardly out of breath.

Lolly shook her head. "We don't know yet," she said. "It'll be up to the producer, I guess."

"Mrs. Sharkey said she was going to call him and find out what he wants," Pop added.

"Until we know, we can't really decide anything," said Lolly. "Sorry."

"But we can decide what we *want* to do," objected Pop, "and then try to get him to agree."

"Okay," said Lolly mildly. "You decide and let me know."

"Lolly!" complained Pop. "This is for *both* of us!"

"Quiet now!" Mr. Penardos said. "You're supposed

to be resting for a moment. What's all this chatter abou'?"

"Pop and Lolly are going to be filmed here at school for a television show," Marmalade told him. "And I was asking if they needed any dancers."

Mr. Penardos laughed. "Oh, yes! I hear abou' this in the staff room. It is exciting," he agreed. "Maybe they will wan' to film this class, in which case we have a lot of work to do."

Danny groaned quietly.

"We can get a routine learn' very quickly if you all work hard, but first we must get you in shape after all the Christmas food you have been eating. Come on. Find a space in the middle of the room. First, withou' music a few times. Arms forward, two, three, four, and *step*..."

The girls were in their room, changing out of their dance clothes, when a girl from the grade above put her head around the door.

"Mrs. Sharkey wants to see you two in her office right away," she told Pop and Lolly.

"Maybe it's about the show!" Pop squealed.

Lolly threw her sweaty T-shirt into the laundry basket and held back the groan she felt like making. "Come on," she said reluctantly. "Let's go and find out."

They made their way over to the main house, and upstairs to the principal's study. Pop knocked on the door, and they both went in.

"I've just had a very interesting discussion with Richard Baslet, the producer of *Kids in the News*," Mrs. Sharkey told them.

Pop trapped her hands between her knees to stop herself from jumping up with excitement.

"It seems this show is going to give Rockley Park a chance to shine, as well as you two. Richard told me he wanted to film you at a modeling assignment, as well as showing singing and other bits and pieces from your normal school day. But when your agent suggested you as subjects for the show, she had to advise him that your mother doesn't like you taking modeling assignments during school time."

Pop's face dropped, but Mrs. Sharkey hadn't finished.

"Don't worry," she said. "Your agent has been in touch with me, too, and between us I think we've come up with a solution." Pop held her breath.

"I told Richard we should be able to arrange some modeling here at Rockley Park," Mrs. Sharkey told the twins. "And he seemed happy with that."

Pop's face lit up. "You mean we can do a fashion show at school, especially for the cameras?" she asked.

Mrs. Sharkey nodded. "Something like that, yes," she agreed.

"Awesome!" Pop yelped, her brain racing. "There are some wooden staging blocks in the dance studio. Could we make them into a catwalk?"

Mrs. Sharkey laughed. "I'm sure we could," she agreed. "Any ideas like that are welcome. Your agent will be coming down tomorrow to discuss the best strategy with you and your teachers."

"Great!" said Pop.

"And I'm hoping there will be an opportunity for

other students in your grade to get involved as well," Mrs. Sharkey added.

"That's good," agreed Lolly seriously. "All our friends will be really happy."

"I'm glad you see it that way," Mrs. Sharkey said. "It shows a generosity of spirit that I have come to expect from you, Polly Lowther." Mrs. Sharkey was so pleased she almost didn't look scary anymore, in spite of her alarming tweed suit.

"Go to see Mr. Player right after the last class tomorrow morning," she told them. "He will help you choose the best song to showcase your talent during the television show. Your agent and Mr. Penardos will meet you there so you can discuss how best to offer Richard Baslet what he wants. This is very exciting for you and the school. Well done, both of you!"

"It's going to be fantastic!" said Pop as they made their way back downstairs. "What should we wear? It's got to be something really stunning."

"Yes," said Lolly. "But hurry up. We're going to be late for chemistry!"

"Who cares!" said Pop airily. "Seeing Mrs. Sharkey was more important than boring old chemistry. Isn't Satin amazing, setting this up?"

"Mmm," muttered Lolly. "Oh, come *on*, Pop. You know how I hate missing the first part of a class."

"Come on, then, nerd," Pop teased. "I'll race you." Together they sprinted downstairs and through the hall. They almost ran headlong into Dave Fallon, the handyman, who was passing through.

"Hey! Watch it!" he yelled as they skirted around him and ran for the door.

"Sorry, Mr. Fallon!" Pop giggled as they passed.

Pop had to endure chemistry and then math before she could tell the others about the meeting with the principal. When at last they filed out of math, she was ready to burst.

"It's going to be wonderful!" she gushed. "And everyone's going to be in it!"

"How come?" asked Chloe.

"Because they want to film parts of our normal school day," Lolly explained more soberly. "So hopefully everyone else will be able to show off their talents, too."

"And we're going to do some modeling, so you all can be the audience!" added Pop.

"Audience?" snorted Tara. "No thanks! What good is that? I'd rather make my *own* arrangements for TV exposure, thank you." She pushed past them and set off alone for the dining room.

"Don't be so snotty!" Pop called after her, but she didn't reply.

"You can't expect Tara to sound grateful," Danny told Pop. "No way will she want to watch while you prance around in front of the cameras!"

"I bet she'll turn up, though," added Marmalade. "Just so she can try to get herself in a shot!"

"Yes," agreed Chloe. "We all want to be on TV, even if it's only for a few seconds."

Everyone agreed with that. How could anyone *not* want to be on TV? But Lolly didn't look so sure.

5. Sleepless

It took Pop a long time to get to sleep that night. Lolly was restless, too. She lay without moving, listening to her twin sister toss and turn. But eventually Lolly heard Pop's breathing become slow and steady. Now the whole room was quiet and only Lolly was still awake.

Lolly had been feeling more and more miserable as the day had progressed. Now she could feel tears welling up, and the effort of holding them in was too much.

It was past midnight. Mrs. Pinto, their housemother and biology teacher, had already been in to check on all the girls and would be back in her own part of the dorm now. Marmalade and Danny were in the boys' dorm at the other side of the school, and even Mr. Timms, who had told the students that he sometimes kept very late hours in his recording studio, must surely have locked up and gone home for the night by now. Apart from the owl Lolly could hear hooting nearby, the whole school was silent. Probably even the horses were dozing in their frosty, moonlit field.

Lolly reached for her bathrobe and slipped quietly out of bed. In bare feet, she made her way cautiously across the floor and out of the door. The buttons of her robe clacked against the handle, and she held her breath and listened. No one stirred. She went to the bathroom and blinked in the strong light. The floor was icy under her bare feet.

She was so miserable her heart felt like a huge stone in her chest. The effort of keeping her unhappiness to herself was exhausting, although she couldn't sleep. She wanted to howl, to let go of the misery that was stifling her, but even now she didn't dare to sob out loud in case anyone heard. She pushed the door of a bath stall open and locked it behind her. It wasn't a very inviting space. At this time of night, the heating had gone off and it was very chilly. Even when she stood on the slatted, wooden bath mat, her toes were still frozen. She doubled her bathrobe beneath her and perched on the side of the empty bathtub. At last, she could let the tears fall.

Lolly had always been easygoing, and happy to follow where her twin sister led. But now she was beginning to realize that this had been a big mistake. Since the girls had come to Rockley Park School, Lolly had seen her life being mapped out in front of her, and it wasn't going the way she wanted. But how could she possibly admit that to her sister, when she was half of the Pop 'n' Lolly act.

Lolly was getting very cold, but she couldn't go back to bed until she'd finished crying, and she felt as if she might cry forever.

Then she heard a sound on the other side of the door. She held her breath. It must be someone needing to use the restroom. Tears were chilling her face, and she longed to wipe them away, but she was afraid to move in case she made a sound and betrayed herself. Surely, in a few moments, whoever it was would go back to bed? She waited for ages, and still no one flushed the toilet. Lolly was getting stiff. She moved one foot slightly, and the wooden mat slid noisily on the hard floor. Then, to her horror, someone knocked on the stall door.

"Lolly? Is that you?" It was Chloe. "Were you crying? Please open the door." Lolly didn't reply, and after a moment Chloe said, "Shall I get Pop?"

Lolly let out a strangled "No!" That was the last thing she wanted.

"You can't stay there all night, Lolly! Let me in, or I'll have to get Mrs. Pinto."

Lolly stayed where she was and tried to decide what was best to do. But her brain had frozen. She was too cold and too tired and too unhappy to think straight.

"Come on, Lolly," said Chloe. There was another pause. "I'm going to wake up Pop, then. She'll know what to do."

Lolly was defeated. She leaned over and unlocked the door. Then she sat back on the side of the empty bathtub and kept her head down so her face was hidden behind her long, glossy hair.

There wasn't much room in the stall, so Chloe crouched beside her and took Lolly's tear-streaked hand in her own. "Come on, Lolly," she said quietly. "What's the matter?"

That did it. Chloe's kindness started her off again.

"You're frozen," Chloe continued. "And I'm cold, too. Don't you want to go back to bed?"

Lolly shook her head.

"Why not?" Chloe asked.

Lolly gulped back her tears for a moment and tried to talk, but all that came out was: "Pop."

"You want me to get Pop?"

Lolly shook her head violently.

"You *don't* want Pop. Why not?"

Lolly shook her head even harder and Chloe squeezed her hand. "All right. We won't wake her," she agreed. "But if you don't want her, will you tell *me* what the matter is?"

Lolly took a deep, wavering breath. Chloe was her best friend, and she was trying to help. But Lolly had thought it was better to keep her troubles to herself.

Chloe *couldn't* help. No one could fix what was troubling her. Even as Lolly thought this, she could feel herself desperately wanting to confide in Chloe. After all, what were friends for if not to help in times of trouble? Although Chloe couldn't make things right, surely Lolly would feel better for sharing her woes? Lolly felt certain she could trust her friend to keep the secret that was causing her so much pain. But would it be fair to burden Chloe with her troubles?

"You must tell *someone*," Chloe insisted while Lolly was still trying to decide. "And it's freezing in here. We'll catch pneumonia! Come on, Lolly. We can't stay here all night!"

"*You* go back to bed, then," said Lolly bravely, trying to sound firm through her tears.

Chloe ignored her. "We need to find somewhere warm where we can talk," she said. "I know!" she added almost at once. "The laundry room! It's always warm in there. Come on, Lolly. We'll go to the laundry room together. No one will hear us. Let's go and get everything figured out."

6. Lolly's Secret

It was hard to argue when you were in floods of tears, and Lolly didn't have the energy to protest any more. So she didn't object too much to being pulled out of the bath stall, and along the corridor to the laundry room. It was a relief not to have to think, and the laundry room *was* invitingly warm.

At one end, there was a big, industrial washing machine and a tumble dryer, as well as racks for drying delicate sweaters and tights. At the other end was a huge, walk-in linen closet with slatted shelves on either side where all the spare bedding was kept.

"Come on," said Chloe. "Let's climb up here. It'll be warm and cozy." She helped Lolly onto a shelf that was half full of sheets, and gave her a stack of pillowcases for her head. Then she eased herself onto the opposite shelf.

It was like being on board a ship, in a cramped cabin. But the piles of sheets were surprisingly comfortable. It was deliciously cozy, too, and there was a soothing smell of clean cotton.

"You're going to have to tell me what's wrong," Chloe said determinedly. "I can't help unless you do."

Lolly's tears threatened to flow again at any moment and she swallowed them back. "You *can't* help me," she said to Chloe.

"I might be able to. Anyway, you shouldn't keep your friends in the dark when you're in trouble. It always helps to talk about things."

"But this is different." Lolly wiped her face and looked at Chloe for the first time. "*You* can't make me want something I don't want. I just can't do it, no matter how hard I try."

"What on earth do you mean?" Chloe looked bewildered.

"You can't make me want to be a pop singer!"

There. She'd said it. But Lolly didn't feel any better. And, by the expression on Chloe's face, she didn't have a clue what Lolly was talking about.

"But…you *do* want to be a singer. That's why you're at Rockley Park…isn't it?"

"It's why *Pop* is here."

"So…Pop wants to sing, but you don't?"

Lolly nodded.

"But why?" said Chloe. "Why come here, then, if you don't want to be in the music industry?"

"You think I'm stupid."

"No!" Chloe objected. "Of course I don't think that. I just don't understand."

Lolly bit her lip and sniffed. "I'm half the act, aren't I?" she said miserably. "And Pop's doing what she's always wanted. I can't let her down. She'd be really upset."

"But *you're* really upset!" reasoned Chloe. "I would *never* do anything I wasn't happy with. My mom wanted me to be something sensible, like a teacher, but I fought and fought to get my scholarship here, and they're really proud of me now! Your feelings are just as important as Pop's. What's so special about her that you have to give in to her all the time? And it's really mean of her to try and make you!"

"No," said Lolly miserably. "She's not making me. That's just it. It's all *my* fault. Pop has no idea I feel like this." Lolly sniffed and took a deep breath. She was going to have to explain it better, or poor Chloe would never understand.

"I've always enjoyed modeling clothes, but I never thought of it as a career," Lolly told Chloe. "Pop is the one who took it seriously. Then, when she said she wanted to try pop singing as well, I didn't mind. I thought that would be fun, too. And it *is* fun," she added. "But everyone at Rockley Park is so serious about making a career in the music industry, and I…I don't want that."

"So what *do* you want to do?" asked Chloe.

Lolly pulled a tissue out of the pocket of her bathrobe and blew her nose. "I hadn't really thought about a career until we came here," she admitted.

"I've known I wanted to sing since I was tiny," said Chloe.

"And Pop's always wanted to be famous," said Lolly. "But by the end of last term, all I knew was that I *didn't* want fame. I thought about it all during vacation, and now that I'm back at school, I figure I'd like to do something with science. Be a doctor, if I can."

"That would be *amazing*!" Chloe said in surprise.

"It would be great if I could do it," Lolly agreed. "But Pop teases me about being good in classes, especially the science ones. She's got no idea how much I love them, and I can't tell her."

"Why not?" Chloe leaned up on one elbow. "I don't see what the problem is."

Lolly gave her a wavering smile. "Because if I follow what *I* want to do, it'll ruin things for Pop. After all, I'm half the act, aren't I? We're not *that* fantastic as singers, but being twins really helps to make us stand out. And Satin promotes us together to take advantage of that. I'm stuck, Chloe, and I don't know what to do."

"Can't you tell your mom?"

"She's spent *years* being proud of her famous twins. She'd be so disappointed in me. I can't tell her."

"Oh, Lolly!" Chloe sounded almost as heartbroken as Lolly felt. "I'm really sorry. I'd hate it so much if I couldn't do what I wanted. You're amazing even to try. I can't think of a way out of this at the moment, but I will. I promise."

Lolly smiled at Chloe's determination. Not *everything* was bad about her life. She couldn't wish for a better friend than Chloe.

But Lolly was worn out with all her crying, and Chloe was tired, too. The warmth in the closet was making them drowsy, and their eyes were beginning to close. Before they knew it, both Lolly and Chloe had slipped into a deep, exhausted sleep.

7. Another Problem

"Chloe. Wake up. It's morning!" said Lolly. She could hear the sound of running water in the bathroom, and early-morning voices. "Come on!"

Chloe rubbed her bleary eyes. "Put those pillowcases back," she mumbled. As quickly as possible, they scrambled off the shelves and straightened the sheets. Then they opened the laundry-room door and went out into the hallway. Tara was on her way to the bathroom.

"What have you been doing?" she asked suspiciously. "I woke up just before the bell and you were both already out of bed."

"Chloe's been helping me look for a sock," Lolly babbled, saying the first thing she could think of.

"Huh!" Tara disappeared for her shower while Lolly and Chloe exchanged glances.

"Phew!" Lolly smiled in relief. "You won't give away what I've told you, will you?" she added in a low voice.

"Of course not. You can trust me," Chloe promised. "Don't worry."

Once Lolly had showered and was on her way to breakfast, she felt much easier in her mind. Her problem hadn't gone away, but sharing it with Chloe *had* helped to make it more bearable. She was even able to listen to Pop's chatter about *Kids in the News* without getting too upset.

After English, she gathered her belongings to follow the others, but Chloe caught her arm.

"Hang on a moment," she said.

"What's the matter?" asked Lolly.

"I've been thinking . . ." Chloe waited until Tara and Marmalade had gone ahead. Pop was chatting with Danny and was well out of hearing range. "If you're serious about wanting to be a doctor, why don't you talk to Mrs. Pinto?"

"Mrs. Pinto? Why?"

"She's a science teacher, isn't she? And she's our

housemother as well. We're supposed to go to her with any problems."

"Yes, but..." Lolly watched Pop disappear out of the room. "She won't be able to help."

"But you could talk to her about being a doctor. You never know, you might not want a science career after you've spoken to her!"

Lolly looked at Chloe doubtfully.

"I don't want to be discouraged."

"I know," said Chloe. "But it might help to talk it over with her anyway. It can't do any harm, and she *might* come up with a good suggestion."

"I'll think about it," Lolly said. "Thanks. Come on. We'd better go and catch up with the others or Pop'll be coming back to look for me in a minute!"

During Mrs. Pinto's biology class, Lolly's mind kept wandering onto what Chloe had said. Should she confide in Mrs. Pinto? What if the teacher told Lolly not to be so stupid as to throw away the chance of success with Pop? After all, this was a school for people who wanted to be musicians, not doctors. Lolly hated not being able to concentrate in biology, which was her favorite subject.

When the bell rang for the end of morning classes, Lolly was slow to collect her things together, but Pop shoved her books into her bag and zoomed toward the door.

"Come on, Loll!" she yelled cheerfully. "Hurry up. Satin will be here!"

Lolly sighed. She'd forgotten Satin was coming for a meeting with Mr. Player and Mr. Penardos.

"Coming!" she said, zipping up her pencil case.

But it wasn't so bad. Satin and the teachers seemed to get along well, and it *was* exciting being the center of attention.

They spent a while discussing what the producer might want. Mr. Penardos thought it would be easy enough to create a catwalk, and Satin was confident about finding exciting clothes for the girls, but Mr. Player was more concerned about what they should sing.

"We don't know if you'll be filmed working on your voices, or singing a whole song," he reminded them.

"But this show is going to be about you trying to break into the pop market, so the choice of song is vital. Your voices aren't the *very* best in the world," he reminded them, "but your presentation is fantastic. What you need is a song that isn't too demanding musically, with a hook that reminds everyone who you are. I think you ought to do 'Dressed to Kill.'"

"Perfect!" said Satin. "That ties in beautifully with your modeling career."

"It would be a good catwalk song," agreed Lolly soberly.

Pop stared at her. "You mean we should sing while we're on the catwalk modeling?"

Lolly shrugged. "If you want."

Pop looked at Mr. Player. "Do you think we could?"

He smiled. "I don't see why not. You're the modeling experts. If you think you can do it, you probably can."

"Well, I think it's a wonderful idea," said Satin enthusiastically. "Good job, Lolly! I'm sure the TV company will go for it. What do you think, Mr. Penardos?"

Mr. Penardos nodded. "I agree with you both," he said. "Bu' we need to think it through. We should choreograph your moves for the best effect."

"We'll need some really cool clothes!" added Pop.

"Yes," agreed Satin. "Let me think about this on the way back to London. I'll speak to a few designers, and we'll see what they come up with."

Pop hugged her twin with glee. "You see!" she said happily. "I said it'd be awesome. And you've come up with the best idea of all. I would never have thought of it, so thank goodness there are two of us!"

8. Hearts and Minds

"We're doing 'Dressed to Kill'!" Pop yelled to Chloe across the hall. She ran over to explain, and as she did so Lolly saw her chance. Pop and Chloe were going into lunch with the others. Pop was so busy telling everyone what had been said about the TV show that she wouldn't notice her sister was missing for a while.

Lolly had decided she didn't want to confide in Mrs. Pinto. She liked her a lot, but she was afraid it all might get too official and out of her control if she involved a teacher. But she *did* think Chloe's idea of finding out more about being a doctor was a good one.

She'd walked past the career room several times, but had never gone in. She had assumed it was for the seniors really. Lolly wasn't sure if it was actually off-limits to the younger students, but it couldn't hurt to have a look.

She sprinted along the hallway and came to a halt outside the door. Nervously, she opened it and went in. The room was empty, so she closed the door behind her and looked around.

Lolly wasn't sure what she had expected, but the career room was a bit of a disappointment. There were lots of heavy books that looked like catalogs, piles of leaflets about drama and music colleges, and a round table with comfortable chairs. It reminded her of a dentist's waiting room. Then she noticed the computer. It was on a desk at the side of the room, and it was switched on.

Lolly went over and touched the mouse. At once, a screen came up with a lot of small, official-looking writing on it. In large letters scrolling across the screen were the words *What do you want to be today?* There was a box to fill in underneath and Lolly couldn't resist. She sat down and typed *Doctor.* Then she clicked the mouse again. *Medicine is one of the most rewarding careers you could choose,* she read.

She felt a glow of pleasure. *But it is one of the most difficult courses of study.*

"I'm good at most subjects," she muttered defiantly, and clicked again.

If you want a career in medicine, you must be prepared to study hard in college and not mind working long hours when you are finally qualified.

"I can do that," Lolly told the computer. She clicked the mouse again.

For an information packet, fill in your details below, invited the computer. Lolly frowned. She didn't really want to fill in her name and address. Her mom had always told her never to give any personal details when she was on the Internet. But surely this would be all right? After all, she was at school, and it looked as if the program had been designed for school use. Probably lots of older students had done it.

Lolly filled all the boxes in very carefully. She put in her proper name, Polly Ann Lowther, and the address of the school. She couldn't remember the school's phone number, but she added her age and waited for the computer to take her to the next page of the program. Nothing happened.

"Darn!" she said to herself. "It's not going to tell me any more until I actually send my details." She thought about it. What if she got into trouble for using the computer without permission? Lolly's hand hovered over the mouse uncertainly. She didn't want to get into trouble, but she really wanted to know more.

She couldn't take a book out of the library because Pop would want to know why she was so interested in medicine all of a sudden. That's if there *were* any books on being a doctor in this library.

But what if she did send her details and the career teacher found out? She probably shouldn't even be in here. She certainly shouldn't be using the computer without permission. And if she got into trouble, Pop would want to know what she'd done.

"Better not," Lolly decided. At that moment the door opened, startling Lolly out of her thoughts. Her hand jerked and the mouse clicked. In a panic, she clicked it again. To her relief, the screen went blank. She must have closed the program down. She turned guiltily to the door, but it was a senior boy, not a teacher.

"Sorry," the boy said. "I didn't mean to make you jump. I was just going to pick up one of those leaflets about the Northern School of Music."

He went over to a shelf and helped himself. "I've never seen anyone your age in here before," he remarked. "You must be very eager!"

Lolly nodded.

"Aren't you one of the model twins?" he added.

"Yes," Lolly admitted.

"I wouldn't have thought *you'd* need career advice!" he said.

"Well, you know . . ." stuttered Lolly. "I was just . . . having a look." But the boy wasn't really interested.

"Bye!" he said, and a moment later he was gone.

Lolly breathed a sigh of relief. She looked at the computer again, but the screen was still blank. It was a pity she hadn't found out very much, but what she had learned certainly hadn't discouraged her from being a doctor. In fact, she felt more determined than ever.

9. Twins at Odds

"What *are* you doing, Lolly?" Pop stared. They were just about to head off for their first class of the day, but her sister was twisting her long hair up and securing it into a tight bun on top of her head.

"What does it look like I'm doing?" Lolly replied. "Fixing my hair."

"But we always wear our hair the same!"

Lolly shrugged. "Well, I felt like a change."

"Why didn't you say so earlier?" Pop protested in a panic. "I haven't got time to do mine like that now."

Lolly smiled at her sister. "We don't have to do *everything* the same, Pop."

"But ... we *always* have our hair down, unless it's for a fashion shoot!" Pop waited for her sister to relent, but

Lolly ignored her. Pop grabbed her bag and stomped off, feeling horrible.

"Lolly is really getting me down," she told Tara on the way to class. "She's in a world of her own half the time. I can't get her to discuss *Kids in the News*, and now look at her hair."

Tara laughed. "What's the matter with it?" she asked.

"It looks ridiculous," Pop told her angrily. "We always wear our hair down. She knows it's our trademark. People will get confused if she starts going around looking like a … a …"

Tara glanced behind them, where Lolly and Chloe were following, deep in conversation. "A crazy dentist?" she suggested.

Pop nodded furiously. "Yes, a crazy dentist is about right. Or an old-fashioned secretary or something. Not like half of Pop 'n' Lolly, anyway."

"Just ignore her," said Tara. "You don't need her around all the time."

Pop looked doubtful. "She's my twin sister," she protested.

"And?" challenged Tara.

"And I don't like it when she starts acting like she's not."

Pop stopped speaking. It was true. It wasn't the fact that Lolly had put her hair up; it was the fact that they hadn't discussed it first that really mattered. If Lolly had suggested it earlier, they would probably have done each other's hair, and giggled while doing it. But Lolly hadn't included her twin. She'd just gone ahead and done it. That's what was so hurtful.

And it got worse for Pop as the day wore on.

"I like your hair!" Danny said to Lolly at break. "It makes you look all grown up."

"Will you help me do mine like that?" teased Marmalade. He grabbed a handful of his long, curly ginger hair and tried to pile it up on the top of his head. Everyone except Pop and Tara giggled.

"I think it makes her look like a crazy dentist," said Tara. But, as usual, everyone ignored her.

Later, there was a singing lesson for the whole class. Every junior high school student had to study singing as well as dance. It meant that as they progressed through the school and specialized more, they would still have a useful working knowledge of those two important skills.

Mr. Player got everyone to sing "Dressed to Kill."

"I'd like you to think about the lyrics," he said to the class. "How can Pop and Lolly get the most out of them? The way lyrics are sung is important. The same words, sung differently, can really change the feel, just as Lolly's sophisticated hairstyle and Pop's casual one are very different, although their actual hair is just the same." Lolly blushed with pleasure and Pop twisted her own, loose hair in her fingers. She wished her hair were up, too. Lolly wasn't the only one who could look sophisticated.

The rest of the class listened while Pop and Lolly ran through the song on their own.

"I'm dressed for my future.

I'm dressed to thrill.

And when you see me out tonight, you'll know

I'm dressed to kill."

"Lovely harmony, girls," Mr. Player said when they'd finished. "You could do with some more volume for the chorus, though. How about if Chloe joins you for those lines?" Chloe grinned happily and joined Pop and Lolly at the piano.

"Yes! That works better," Mr. Player told them. "Let's run through it one more time."

Pop thought hard about the words she and Lolly were singing.

Dressed to kill, she brooded. *That's what Lolly is with her hair like that! Why is she making herself look different? She's never tried to upstage me before, but she is now. I'm her twin! How can she do this to me?*

10. Dressed to Kill

"Find a space an' lie down on your backs," Mr. Penardos told the class, when they arrived later at the dance studio. He put on some soothing music. "Close your eyes," he said, "an' concentrate on breathing. Empty your minds an' jus' breathe. In an' out, in an' out."

Pop couldn't relax. She hoped Lolly would have to undo her hair so she could rest her head on the floor properly, but Lolly's hair was fine. She lay near her twin with her eyes closed, looking serene, breathing regularly.

"You're not concentrating, Pop," Mr. Penardos said. "Relax your whole body an' really listen to the music. In an' out, in an' out. That's better."

By the time they had progressed through all the loosening-up exercises, Lolly's hair was looking a bit wispy, but Mr. Penardos still liked it enough to compliment her.

"This style is de rigueur for most ballet classes," he told everyone. "An' you can see why the teachers insist on it. Look at the shape of Lolly's head, neck, and shoulders. In classical ballet, the way you hold your head and shoulders is very importan', but with your hair down the effect is blurred. Very nice, Lolly. Thank you." He glanced briefly at Pop and then away again. Pop felt as if she'd been horribly snubbed.

"I think we do a dance routine to 'Dressed to Kill,'" Mr. Penardos went on, putting the CD into his player.

Tara groaned. "Honestly!" she muttered to Danny. "I'm fed up with 'Dressed to Kill.' I can't wait for my individual bass lesson."

"This will be a useful class exercise in cooperation," Mr. Penardos explained, ignoring Tara's grumbles.

Then he asked Lolly to demonstrate how to move like a model.

He only chose her because of her hair, Pop thought resentfully. *He should have asked us both to do it.*

Mr. Penardos wanted everyone to follow Lolly up and down an imaginary catwalk as part of the routine.

"No, no!" he said to Tara. "You look as if you're marching off to battle, not modeling clothes! Marmalade's got it. Look!" Marmalade had indeed got it, but being Marmalade, his take on a model's walk was rather too exaggerated, and hugely funny. Everyone except Pop, Marmalade, and Tara burst into laughter.

"What's the matter?" asked Marmalade, struggling to keep a straight face, knowing full well that he had mimicked Lolly to a tee. Lolly looked as if she were enjoying the fun as much as the rest of the class, but Pop felt even more left out.

Tara stalked over to a chair in the corner, sat down, and fumed.

"Come on, Tara," Mr. Penardos coaxed her. "You mus' admit. It was ver' funny."

Tara ran her hands impatiently through her short,

black hair. "That's just it!" she said. "No one takes anything seriously around here! Mr. Player said to think about the words, but has that altered the way they perform the song? No! They sing it as if they're on a trip to the seashore!"

"Well!" Mr. Penardos said, smiling at Tara. "And have you told Mr. Player any of this?"

Tara shrugged. "No point." She looked at Pop for a moment. "It's not *my* problem."

"It *would* be good if there was a bit of an edge to the song," said Danny.

"Anyone else?" asked Mr. Penardos.

"I like the dance we're working out," ventured Marmalade. "But we could be more menacing. Be gangsters perhaps."

"Like in *Bugsy Malone*," Chloe suggested.

"An' what do Pop 'n' Lolly have to say about these ideas?" asked Mr. Penardos.

"They sound good," Pop agreed quickly, before Lolly could say anything.

"I don't know if our voices would be suited to making

the song sound very different, but we could ask Mr. Player, couldn't we?" Lolly suggested to her twin.

Pop ignored her and spoke directly to Mr. Penardos. "Mr. Player suggested the song," she said. "So he must have thought we could handle it."

"This exercise is throwing out some interesting ideas," said Mr. Penardos, sounding pleased. "Shall I try to set up a joint lesson with Mr. Player? Perhaps we could even merge the singing and dance classes while we work on this."

Everyone agreed enthusiastically.

"Okay! Let's finish now. You're doing well. Give 'Dressed to Kill' lots of thought, an' come next time with more ideas. You know we're trying to come up with something for Pop 'n' Lolly that the *Kids in the News* people will like. We can't guarantee they'll use any of it, but who knows? If it goes really well, maybe you'll *all* find yourselves on TV!"

11. Song and Dance

The next day, Lolly and Chloe were able to have a quick conversation in the laundry room while Pop was busy putting her hair up like Lolly had the day before.

"I thought about what you said about talking to Mrs. Pinto," Lolly told Chloe. "But I decided I could maybe find out something about being a doctor by myself."

"How?" asked Chloe.

"Well, I went and had a look in the career room."

Chloe looked impressed. "That was a good idea," she said. "I didn't realize we were allowed to go there whenever we wanted."

"I'm not sure we are," Lolly admitted.

"So, did you find anything interesting?"

Lolly shook her head. "Not enough. I'll need to go back and have another look. But what I saw definitely didn't discourage me. I still want to try to be a doctor if I can." She hesitated. "I might be better going to a more academic school, though, to help me get good enough grades."

Chloe's eyes widened. "You mean leave Rockley Park? Really?"

"I don't know," Lolly told her. "Maybe. I hope not. I like it here. But I might have to." She smiled ruefully. "Pop won't be very happy if I have to leave."

"She'll go ballistic!" agreed Chloe. "But you must stand up to her if it's what you really want."

"I will," Lolly told her. "I know I've been silly giving in to her so much. But that's all going to change now that I've found something that really matters to me. Trouble is, although she shouts and has tantrums, she's not as tough as she makes out. She relies on me so much."

"Really?" said Chloe. "I didn't realize that."

"I know everyone thinks she's the boss," said Lolly. "But she's nothing near as strong as me underneath.

She's quite insecure really. That's the trouble with being a twin. If you're not careful, you can find yourself being half a person instead of a whole one. She's been able to prance around and make a fuss as much as she likes because she knows I'll always be the calm, quiet one for her."

"Twins at my last school were split up and put into different classes," Chloe said thoughtfully.

"I wish *our* last school had done that," said Lolly. "Pop *couldn't* have insisted we do everything the same if it had."

Lolly pulled one of her fleece tops off the drying rack and folded it up.

"Pop's so intent on us being identical that she's not thinking properly," she said. "What's going to happen when we want boyfriends? Will we have to wait until we meet twin boys that we both like?" She frowned. "I can't live like that."

"So what are you going to do?" asked Chloe.

"I'm just going to do my own thing," said Lolly. "I think that's all I *can* do. Pop didn't like me having my hair different from hers, but I hope she will get used to me making changes."

"She's putting *her* hair up now, though," Chloe reminded Lolly. "You'll both be the same again. And I think she's going to be watching you like a hawk every time you get your hairbrush out!"

"She'll get tired of being a copycat," Lolly said. "She hasn't got the patience for it. And I know how much she loves having her hair loose. She always makes a fuss when we have to have it styled for fashion shoots. Eventually she'll *have* to realize that we don't always need to look identical and then maybe she'll get used to the idea that it's okay if our lives go in different directions, too.

"Come on," she added, looking at her watch. "Let's go and find her. We'll be late for class if we don't hurry."

The next afternoon, everyone gathered in the dance studio for a joint dance and singing session. Mr. Penardos had built a catwalk out of the large, wooden staging blocks, and he and Mr. Player were discussing how best to bring the singing and modeling together.

"I think the rest of the class can be more involved than simply being an audience," said Mr. Player.

Mr. Penardos nodded. "I agree," he said. "Marmalade suggested gangsters, and the dance we've been working on does have that feel now. The gangsters come toward the catwalk to threaten the models, but Pop 'n' Lolly are more than a match for them with their rendering of 'Dressed to Kill.' Do you think that will work?"

"Certainly. Let's give it a try."

Pop wanted to squeal with excitement, but with her hair piled up like Lolly's she was eager to appear as sophisticated as her sister had. She contented herself with a powerful grin at Chloe instead.

"We ought to start," Mr. Player added. "Where's your sister?" he asked Pop. "It's not like either of you to be late."

Pop shrugged. "She said she'd be along in a few minutes," she told the voice coach awkwardly. She felt embarrassed at not knowing what was keeping her twin sister.

Just then, the door opened and Lolly came in. Pop felt herself blush with anger and confusion. What on earth was Lolly up to? Only a few minutes before, her hair had been up like Pop's, but now it was in stupid bunches, with red, feathered hairbands holding it in place.

"Er… I thought we were going to give this song some menace," said Mr. Penardos in an embarrassed voice. "Aren't we going for a gangster look, Pop?"

Pop glared at the teacher in disgust. "She's Lolly, not Pop," she told him. "*I'm* Pop!" And then, unaccountably, she felt hot tears slide down her face. Mr. Penardos had thought Lolly, with her hair in silly bunches, was her! Didn't he think she was able to look sophisticated? It was *so* unfair. Before she could embarrass herself any more, Pop bent her head and ran out of the door. Everyone looked at one another awkwardly. What on earth was going on?

"Sorry," muttered Lolly. "I'll go and bring her back."

After a few minutes she found Pop in the girls' restroom. "What's the matter?" she asked.

"As soon as I make my hair like yours, you change it again," she accused Lolly through her tears. "Why are you being so mean? And Mr. Penardos got us mixed up, even though I would *never* put *my* hair in bunches."

"I didn't mean to upset you this much." Lolly sighed. "I'm sorry."

"So how much *did* you mean to upset me? I'm your *sister*," wailed Pop. "Why are you trying to upstage me?"

"I'm not," Lolly protested. "I'm just trying to be myself."

But Pop wasn't listening. "Well, it won't work," she sniffed. "I'm just as good a model as you, and I'll be just as good a pop singer. I won't let you steal the limelight during *Kids in the News*, because I know how to be a true professional, and you don't." Pop wiped her red eyes angrily and flung open the door. "Get a move on. We've got a class to go to." Pop stalked out of the bathroom and back to the dance studio.

"Come on now, Pop," Mr. Player said, getting her name right. "Don't act up just because Mr. Penardos got you and Lolly confused for a moment."

Pop and Lolly both apologized, but Pop wouldn't

meet Lolly's eyes and the atmosphere in the room was very uncomfortable.

"You should be able to give this song more bite," Mr. Player went on. "Get some real venom in your voice when it comes to the word *kill*. There's a pause after *tonight,* so make sure you take a breath then, so you can really build *kill*. I know it's not a crescendo, but you're supposed to sound menacing, so don't swallow that last word. Let's run through it one more time."

Pop concentrated on how angry she was with Lolly. They sang again and Mr. Player nodded.

"Better. Much better. I had thought you wanted to keep it light, and concentrate on the clothing aspect of the song because of your modeling, but it works very well this way. Now. We've got Chloe's powerful voice bringing a lot of drama to the chorus, but I think we could do with a much more moody intro to the song. Any ideas for how we can accomplish that?"

"Tara is always moody," suggested Marmalade. Everyone laughed and the awkwardness from the twins' tiff was broken.

"Actually, I think you have a good idea, Marmalade," Mr. Penardos said. "Tara, you an' Danny are not the best dancers, but you play drums an' bass. Could you come up with a bluesy intro to the song?"

Danny and Tara exchanged pleased glances. "Yes!" they agreed.

"So. We can have you both brooding *here*," Mr. Penardos said to the two musicians, "at the bottom of the catwalk we've built. Tara, you will be in your usual black, naturally. Danny, can you ask the art depar'ment to come up with some painted bullet holes for your bass drum?"

"Cool idea!" said Danny. "And I'll wear my black drumming gloves. Chloe always says they make me look menacing!"

"Now, Pop 'n' Lolly can do their stuff on the catwalk as the first verse begins. You gangsters come to meet them, an' the twins cut them dead. Let's do another run-through."

It was looking good. This was what it was all about. Pop 'n' Lolly in action, doing what they did best.

"Keep it going!" Mr. Penardos yelled as they tried a run-through again. "Your cue, Pop...an' *now*! Gangsters!"

As the twins finished the chorus with Chloe, the gangster dancers confronted the girls on the catwalk again. Pop and Lolly turned with a flourish and cut the gangsters dead.

Mr. Penardos and Mr. Player clapped. "Well done, all of you," said Mr. Player. "Off you go now or you'll be late for your next class."

Pop pulled the pins out of her hair and let it fall loosely over her shoulders as normal. She shot her sister a baleful glance. Maybe it wasn't such a good idea to play catch-up with hairstyles. Nothing would induce her to wear feathery, red hairbands. But Lolly was behaving oddly, very oddly indeed, and Pop didn't like it one bit.

12. Lolly Spills the Beans

The next day, there was an assembly in the theater. Mrs. Sharkey had an important announcement for the whole school.

"A television crew will be filming here later this week," she said. Everyone sat up and paid more attention. So the rumors that had been flying around were true!

"The crew will be filming for the *Kids in the News* series, which will feature Pop 'n' Lolly Lowther."

Lots of students were exchanging excited glances.

"They will film some of the school day for the show and part of a catwalk performance the class has been rehearsing."

Several members of their grade, including Marmalade, punched the air in triumph and whooped. Mrs. Sharkey glared at them until they quieted down again. Pop and Lolly smiled at each other, their differences forgiven for the moment.

"A roving cameraman will be here at ten o'clock tomorrow," Mrs. Sharkey continued. "And a whole crew will be in the dance studio the following afternoon for the performance and some interviews, so the studio will be off-limits that day for all except those involved in the filming. I would like to make it clear that no one is to disturb the film crew, follow them around, or in any way make their work more difficult than it already is. They have asked that everyone ignore their presence as much as possible, and I'll expect you all to do just that."

As Lolly and Pop and their friends filed out of the theater, there was an excited buzz of conversation around them.

"Yeah!" yelped Marmalade. It was hard to spin around on one leg in such a crush of students, but somehow he managed it without knocking into too many people.

"Way to go!" said a senior girl who Lolly knew had just signed a recording contract.

"Way to go to you, too," Lolly replied. The girl looked startled for a moment and then blushed.

"Oh, yes!" she said, her face lit up with happiness. "Isn't it wonderful when everything goes right for you?" She pushed her way through the crowd and disappeared. Lolly stood and watched her go, wishing she felt as happy as that.

Beside Lolly, Pop was holding court to a series of admirers. "It's the combination of modeling and singing that hooked the TV company," she was saying. "Lots of people try to cross over from one thing to another, but not many make it convincingly. We hope that coming here will help us realize our dream."

She was good; Lolly had to hand it to her. Pop sounded so self-assured and grown up when she was in the spotlight. She was only talking to other students, but she could have been doing an interview for television already. They might be identical twins, but while Pop behaved every inch the glamorous celebrity, Lolly certainly didn't feel like one.

She noticed Chloe in the crush. "Coming back to our room?" she asked, once she'd managed to join her friend.

"Okay."

The crowd was thinning out as students went to collect their books and go on to their classes.

"I wish I could give you my role in this TV thing," Lolly said as they made their way along the path to the dorm.

"Never mind," said Chloe. "You'll enjoy it while it's happening."

"Yes," Lolly admitted. "I suppose I will, but it all makes me feel as if I'm on a runaway bus and I can't get off."

"Frosty day, frosty faces!" exclaimed Pop, running to catch up to them on the crunchy gravel walk. "Don't worry. You'll both be fine! Just ignore the camera, Chloe. It won't be on you much anyway." She turned to Tara and the gaggle of other girls coming along behind. "Take two," she said, pretending to film them. "After a healthy breakfast, the girls go to collect their books for their first class!"

At lunchtime, a package arrived for the twins. Chloe and Tara watched as they unpacked the clothes that had been sent for the filming. Satin had done well.

"Wow! Look at it all," said Chloe as two suits, loads of different tops, and various skirts and pairs of jeans were revealed. "Why do you need so many clothes?"

"So we can choose," explained Lolly. "The suits are for the performance," she added, reading a note from Satin. "She thought they would be good for the gangster look."

"Louis Rose," said Pop, opening one of the jackets and showing Tara the designer label. "My favorite, and horrendously expensive. Too bad we won't be able to keep them."

"Why not?" asked Chloe.

"Designers don't give away this sort of stuff every day," Pop told her.

"The casual wear is all from Ginger-Fizz," read Lolly. "Satin says we should choose something we really like out of the selection to wear during the day. Oh! And Ginger-Fizz says we can keep one outfit each as long as we wear it rather than give it away!"

"It's not couture, you see," Pop explained. "You can get this label easily in regular stores. And I figure they think they'll get more sales if kids see us wearing their clothes."

Tara sniffed at the bright colors of the outfits. "Huh!" she said, poking a vivid green top derisively. "You wouldn't catch me wearing *that*."

"That's because you only wear black!" Pop laughed.

"It doesn't say anything about not *lending*," Lolly said. "How about this, Chloe? Do you like it?" Chloe nodded enthusiastically at the gorgeously soft cashmere sweater in bubblegum pink. "I'll keep this one, then," Lolly continued. "I *will* wear it, but you can borrow it anytime you like, Chloe."

Lunchtime was spent trying on clothes, but all too soon the bell rang for afternoon classes.

"Come on, we'd better put this all away," said Pop. "Have you got any space in your closet, Chloe? Mine's stuffed full!"

That evening, Pop, Lolly, and Chloe were sitting on their beds discussing the arrival of the film crew the next day.

"Now you're not going to do anything stupid with your hair tomorrow, are you?" Pop said to Lolly. "I know Satin would want us to wear it in our trademark style, just loose, over our shoulders. If you want to do anything else," she added, "let's talk about it now."

"It's not my hair that bothers me," mumbled Lolly.

Pop frowned. "What does, then?" she asked. "Well?" she demanded. "Go on."

Lolly looked into her sister's eyes. She saw them widen as Pop realized something serious was up. Lolly's heart started to beat faster.

I could say it was just nerves or something, she told herself. *I don't have to admit what's really wrong. I don't want to upset her.* She looked at Chloe, sitting quietly on her bed. They exchanged a quick glance and then Chloe looked away, but it was enough to give Lolly courage.

This is stupid, she thought. *It's about me! About what I want! And it's important. It's not possible to do this gently.*

Pop was waiting, her eyes looking frightened now. "What?" she asked. "What's wrong?"

Lolly tossed back her hair and firmly lifted her chin. "I don't want to be famous anymore," she said.

13. Blown Apart

Pop's mouth dropped open. She stared at Lolly.

"What do you mean, you don't want to be famous anymore!"

Lolly stood up and started pacing up and down, her heart racing.

"It's not the fame so much. I enjoyed all that to start with," she babbled. "But I don't want to be a model or a pop singer forever. There are other things I'd rather do."

"What things?" asked Pop faintly.

"It's fun being a model, but there's more to life," Lolly continued. "And the longer I'm at school here, the more I realize I don't want to be a pop singer, either. It's . . . it's shallow."

There was a gasp from Chloe, and Lolly realized she'd gone much too far.

"How DARE you!" yelled Pop. "How dare you say such a thing! What about all the enjoyment pop singers bring to their fans? What about all the charity things tons of pop singers and models do? Is that shallow? IS it?"

Lolly shook her head. "No," she said. "I didn't mean . . ."

"No one knows what you mean!" shouted Pop. "I used to, but not anymore. I don't know what you think you're doing, but I don't believe a word you're saying. You've never even given me a *hint* that you don't like what we do. Why wait until now? Don't you think it's a bit strange that you should wait until we're just about to have the chance of our lives before you make a fuss?"

Pop's furious expression had distorted her face into a frightening mask.

"You're *jealous* of me because I work so hard at what we do," she shouted at Lolly. "You've always just tagged along behind, and now you're afraid I'll outshine you tomorrow. You don't want that. Oh no! It would never work for me to be better than you at anything, would it?"

"But . . ."

"You've been trying to upset me, haven't you? So I won't do well in front of the cameras. But you wait." Pop thrust her face close to her sister's. "Just you wait." Pop was breathing deeply, almost snarling with fury. "I'll show you how professional I can be. I'll *shine* in front of the cameras, and I'll shine as a singer, however hard you try to stop me."

There was silence in the room. Then Pop let out a choking gulp. Grabbing a jacket from her chair, she flung open the door and ran straight into Tara, who was coming in. Pop pushed her roughly aside and disappeared at a run down the hallway.

"Well!" said Tara conversationally. "Should I go after her?"

Chloe looked at Lolly, but Lolly had sunk onto her bed and was lying with her face in her pillow.

Tara shrugged. "Perhaps I will, then," she said, and slipped back out of the room.

Chloe went over to Lolly's bed. "Lolly?" she said tentatively.

Lolly rolled over and sat up. Her eyes were red, and she looked utterly miserable.

"I'm sorry for saying what I did about pop singers," she said in a whisper. "I didn't mean it. And it's not true. There are shallow people and good people in almost every job."

"I know," said Chloe.

"But I got so angry. Angry with myself really, for getting into this position. I didn't say anything right, and now Pop's got totally the wrong impression. She's no nearer to realizing what I want and we've had a terrible argument for nothing. What *am* I going to do?"

"I should have stopped Tara," said Chloe. "She'll only make things worse."

"There's no point in *me* going after Pop while she's like this," Lolly said in a small voice. "I'd just upset her again. The best thing for me is to leave her alone until she cools down."

There was no more to be said. Quietly, Lolly and

Chloe got ready for bed. By the time they'd finished in the bathroom, there was still no sign of Pop or Tara.

"Do you think they're all right?" asked Chloe.

"I hope so," said Lolly. "They couldn't have gone far. It'll be time for lights-out soon."

"Should I go and see if they're in the downstairs common room?" Chloe suggested.

Lolly nodded. "Do you mind?"

But Chloe didn't need to go. Just then the door opened and Pop came in with Tara. Pop tossed a large, white envelope on her bed and undressed in silence with her back to Lolly while Tara went to the bathroom.

As soon as she was in her pajamas, Pop picked up the envelope and began to tear it open. But now Lolly could see what was written on the front of it, and she was appalled at what she saw.

"No!" she shouted in horror. "No! Don't open it!"

Pop stared at her sister for a moment and then looked away. She had had more than enough of Lolly's weird behavior. Just to make sure, she glanced at the name on the envelope again. *Miss P. Lowther.* It was definitely for her. Though what a career service wanted to send her information for, she couldn't imagine. *Another Information Pack from careers@whatdoyouwanttobe.com* was splashed all over the front of the envelope.

"Don't," begged Lolly in agony, but Pop ignored her. She ripped open the envelope and pulled out the contents. A photograph of a cheery woman in a white coat smiled up at her. SO YOU WANT TO BE A DOCTOR! the headline said above the picture.

No, I don't, thought Pop impatiently. *How stupid.* She riffled through the bundle of leaflets and found a cover letter. As she began to read it, time seemed to stand still.

Dear Polly Lowther, it said. Polly, not Pop. Polly was Lolly's real name. They'd been christened Poppy and Polly. Only later had they picked up the nicknames that had stuck. *Dear Polly.* The letter was for Lolly! But why? Why did she want information about being a doctor?

Pop glanced up at her sister and her blood ran cold. It was there, in Lolly's ashen face. The truth. Lolly wanted to be a doctor, not a pop singer. She didn't want to upstage Pop. It was worse than that. Far worse.

Pop picked up the contents of the letter with trembling hands and went over to Lolly's bed. She felt as if she might faint, or be sick, but somehow she managed to drop the information onto her sister's bed. Then she put her hand up to her mouth and walked very carefully to the door. She didn't know where she could go, but she couldn't bear to stay there. She fumbled for the handle and let herself out.

It wasn't long before Mrs. Pinto came to tell them that Pop had gone over to the infirmary.

"Don't worry," Mrs. Pinto said. "I'm sure she'll be fine in the morning. I expect it's just a few jitters before the camera crew arrives tomorrow. Are you all right?" she asked Lolly.

"Yes," said Lolly untruthfully.

Mrs. Pinto didn't seem to notice Lolly's wobbly voice. She simply switched off their light and said a cheery good night.

Lolly was certain she wouldn't sleep at all, and it felt as if she'd tossed and turned all night. When it was time to get up she felt groggy, and very unready to face a camera.

"Pop will be well enough to join you for the filming," Mrs. Pinto told Lolly when she went down to ask. "She's sending a note over."

Lolly breathed a sigh of relief. Pop must have calmed down. Everything would be all right.

"It's probably for the best," Chloe said when Lolly went back upstairs. "At least Pop knows the truth now. But it must have been a terrible shock to find out by reading your mail. I didn't know you'd sent out for information on being a doctor."

"Neither did I!" Lolly said. "I'd filled in my address on the screen, but I wasn't sure about sending it. Then someone came in and made me jump. I jerked the mouse and the next thing I knew the screen was blank.

I must have clicked send, but I didn't even realize the career computer was actually online."

"You're not supposed to give personal details to *anyone* online," Tara told her.

"I know," said Lolly. "And I won't do it again. I've learned my lesson, that's for sure."

A hall monitor arrived with the note from Pop just before they had to go to breakfast. Lolly sat down to read it while Chloe and Tara hovered nearby.

Lolly, I hate you for breaking up our duo. Why did you agree to come to this school if you hate singing so much? I especially hate you for letting me find out the way you did. What am I supposed to do when you run off to college and leave me all alone?

But a professional performer never lets anything get in the way of a performance and I won't let your deceit ruin today. I will be

*there for the filming, but don't
expect me ever to speak to you again.*

*Call Mom as soon as possible and
get her to send you to a different
school. If you don't want to be part
of Pop 'n' Lolly, I don't want you
here, spoiling everything.*

Poppy Lowther

A sob broke out of Lolly's throat. Her twin sister, her best friend, the person she loved more than anyone, wanted her out of her life.

"What does she say?" asked Chloe anxiously.

Wordlessly, Lolly handed her the note and Chloe read it.

"Well?" demanded Tara.

Lolly waved her hand. "You might as well read it, too," she said hopelessly. "Everyone is going to know sooner or later."

Tara read the note, folded it up, and gave it back to Lolly.

"Pop's right," she said flatly.

Chloe turned on her. "Tara! How could you?"

"She's right about being professional," Tara explained. "The most important thing to do is to get through the filming. You can figure out everything else later."

Lolly tried very hard to be as professional as her sister. The camerawoman followed them from class to class, and after a while it was almost possible to forget she was filming them. She shot Lolly discussing her work with Mrs. Pinto, and she got a lot of film of Pop and Tara chatting and laughing together.

"I'm not getting much of you two together," the camerawoman complained to the twins, so Pop took her sister's arm and strolled with her beside the lake, the cold air causing misty puffs of breath to form as Pop made bright conversation and Lolly fumbled for something interesting to say. As soon as the shot was finished, Pop disengaged her arm and ignored Lolly again.

"I see you're not inseparable, like some twins," the camerawoman observed drily.

"Oh no!" Pop agreed in a falsely bright voice. "It's important to have lots of friends. We can't always rely on each other. That would be silly!"

Lolly wilted even more after that and the day dragged on and on. But when the camerawoman eventually left, Lolly gathered up her courage and made a point of cornering her sister.

"I'm really sorry I've upset you," she said. "Can we talk about it and try to make up?"

Pop stared at her twin coldly and didn't even bother to reply.

Nothing had changed by bedtime. Lolly peeled off the gorgeous, bubblegum-pink sweater she'd been wearing and put it on the end of Chloe's bed. But although she was pleased to lend it to Chloe, she couldn't feel enthusiastic about anything else at the moment.

"For goodness' sake!" complained Tara as she climbed into bed. "I thought *I* was supposed to be the grumpy one, but you two are grumpy enough for the whole country!"

It was unusual for Tara to try to make people laugh, and at any other time it would have been funny, but tonight no one was in the mood.

"Shut up, Tara," said Chloe. "Sorry," she added after a moment.

"Let's just get some sleep," Lolly said miserably. "The camera crew will be here to film the performance tomorrow. And it's going to be a big day."

14. Lights, Camera, Action!

In the morning, things were as bad as ever between Pop and Lolly. But there was no time to mope. Marmalade and Danny came racing into breakfast with some exciting news.

"The camera crew is here!"

Almost everyone leaped to their feet and went to the window. Sure enough, a large white truck was parked on the grass by the dance studio and several people in jeans and jackets were carrying masses of equipment indoors.

The class still had to endure their first two classes, in spite of all the excitement. Not a lot of work got done, and by break time everyone was in a fever of anticipation. At the end of break, they were all asked to gather in the main hall. Mr. Penardos was there with Mr. Player.

"The producer would like to see you do a run-through first so he knows where to position his cameras," Mr. Penardos announced. "Bu' before we do tha' we need to get you changed and into makeup. Can we have Pop an' Lolly first, please? Then the res' of you can come through."

Pop and Lolly were used to being made up for modeling. "I'll just give you a bit of powder, mascara, and some neutral lipstick," the makeup artist told them. "Your agent thinks a simple look would be best, to emphasize your youth." She was very quick, and in no time the twins were going through to the dance studio.

It had been transformed during the morning. Black power cables snaked all over the floor. All the blinds were down, shutting out the gray morning light, and there were artificial lights on tall stands everywhere. Three large black cameras waited, ready to roll, with their cameramen nearby. An extraordinary number of people were busy, rushing here and there, carrying clipboards or speaking into radios.

Pop and Lolly were going to be up on the catwalk soon, doing their stuff. And somehow, although Lolly had appeared in lots of fashion shows in front of hundreds of people, this was even more scary. Was it the cameras, or performing in front of their friends? Lolly didn't think it was either of those things. She knew she felt this way because she and her sister were going to be working closely together as always, and yet they had never been so far apart.

Satin was sitting on a folding chair, speaking earnestly to a harassed-looking man in a Hawaiian shirt. As the twins hesitated, a younger man rushed up to them and checked their names on his clipboard.

"I'm Hugh, the floor manager," he said. "And this is our producer, Richard." The Hawaiian shirt man turned away from Satin for a moment and nodded at Pop and Lolly. "Can you take your starting positions, please?" asked Hugh. "When everyone's ready, Richard will make some decisions about the cameras."

The producer took ages discussing angles with the cameramen, moving the lights a few inches one way or another, but everyone was so interested they didn't mind the wait. Even Tara chatted excitedly with Danny while the producer peered through the lens of one large camera that was mounted on a sort of crane.

Together on the catwalk, Pop and Lolly were the only ones who weren't chatting. It was killing Lolly, the way Pop was managing to cut her dead while giving the impression that she was on perfectly good terms with her sister. If only Pop would glance at her just once, and show that she was going to forgive her eventually, it would help. But Pop was looking everywhere except at her sister, and Lolly was getting more and more upset. She was even finding the heat of the lights difficult to handle, although catwalk lights had never bothered her in the past. The makeup artist had to climb up onto the catwalk twice with her powder puff to take the shine off Lolly's face.

If only Pop would talk to Lolly. Even another blazing

argument might clear the air a bit. But the last thing they could do was fight in front of the cameras.

Once everything was in place, they had to do a run-through, but simply by pacing out the performance, rather than singing and dancing it. Richard kept stopping them in the middle of a verse, or a gangsters' approach, and it got terribly confusing. But everyone looked great. The school wardrobe mistress had done everyone proud, and Pop and Lolly's designer suits looked fantastic.

After everything was set up perfectly, the producer and floor manager had a few minutes' discussion and then Richard went and sat down in the shadows at the back of the room.

"Richard wants you to come in chatting," said Hugh. "As if you've just arrived for a dress rehearsal. Brilliant idea, by the way, to blend the catwalk action with a song."

Hugh got the thumbs-up from the cameramen, the lighting crew, and the soundman with his overhead microphone on a long boom. "Quiet, please. Cameras rolling," announced Hugh. "Action." And then he retreated behind the lights with his clipboard to join the producer.

Lolly couldn't think of a thing to say, but Pop chattered away as if she was quite happy.

"I really like these suits!" she said, grinning at a point just past Lolly's ear. "Are you going to be able to walk in the shoes?"

"Yes," replied Lolly automatically, thinking how quick Pop had been in mentioning the designer clothes they'd been lent. If that part wasn't cut from the final film, the designer would be thrilled, and send more work their way. Pop really was a true professional.

Danny counted Tara in by tapping his drumsticks and they began their intro. Pop 'n' Lolly started to sing the first verse and strutted their way down the catwalk to where Chloe was waiting.

Lolly was straining every cell in her body just to get through, but Pop was milking the song for all she was worth. By the time the twins got to Chloe, Pop was unstoppable.

To Lolly's surprise, her sister linked arms with her, but it wasn't a sisterly maneuver. Her grip was tight, and Lolly realized that Pop had remembered the incident with Tikki Deacon and was leaving nothing to chance.

"I'm dressed for my future.
I'm dressed to thrill.
And when I see your eyes, you'll know
I'm dressed to kill."

Three girls were singing the chorus, but it might as well have been Pop alone. As she sang the last six words, she fixed Lolly with such a look of hatred that Lolly stopped singing entirely. Then Pop threw her sister's arm away from her and stalked back up the catwalk alone, singing the second verse. Lolly couldn't help it; she looked totally beaten as she dragged after Pop.

Please don't, Lolly begged her sister silently behind her back. *Please don't hate me so much. I can't bear it. I never wanted to hurt you, but I'm important, too.*

And then it happened. Lolly got angry as well.

She lifted her head defiantly, and strode after her sister. She was just in time to join Chloe and Pop in the second chorus. She knew Pop would be looking straight into camera one, so she stood in front of it for a moment so that she and Pop were face-to-face. She didn't need to feel so guilty. This was something they *both* had to work out.

Pop couldn't avoid looking deep into Lolly's eyes. It was enough. That single glance brought Pop up short. Her sister's dilemma seared into her brain and she finally understood. Pop faltered. Then her professionalism kicked in again. But she was different, more hesitant, and although she wouldn't look at Lolly again, Lolly was certain she was thinking of *them* now, not just the song.

It was strange not having any applause at the end. And Lolly was conscious of Satin's anxious face. But the producer and his staff were thrilled.

"Wow! Amazing stuff!" whooped Richard. The camera crew and the rest of the technicians smiled. "That was some feisty performance, young lady,"

Richard said to Pop, beaming from ear to ear. "Have you considered acting as a career? And that look between you, in the second chorus! Did we get that on camera two? Fantastic! You *all* did really well," he added to the class.

It was time for a final interview and Hugh was asking the questions off camera. When the film was edited, it would sound as if the girls were talking right to the audience instead of replying to the out-of-sight floor manager.

"Our mother sent a photograph of us to the agent Satin Fountain-Blowers," said Lolly in answer to a "how did you get started?" question. "She took us on when we were really little, something like six, I think. I can't remember what our first modeling job was."

"I can," said Pop. "I can remember every moment. It was for a catalog, and we wore tons of different things. I remember that there were several other kids doing it as well, and some got really fed up. Lolly got quite tired, but *I* loved it all."

"Satin suggested we audition for Rockley Park

School," Pop continued in answer to another off-camera question. "We'd always enjoyed singing, and she thought it would be a good idea to gain some experience in another field. I'd always wanted to be a pop singer," she continued wistfully, "with my sister..."

Lolly looked down and concentrated on a thread in the skirt of her suit. She could feel her heart pounding. What was Pop up to now? Did she intend to totally humiliate her on camera?

Pop gazed into the camera earnestly, as only Pop Lowther could. "But I don't think she'll be around to sing with me when we're grown up."

Her revelation had the floor manager puzzled. He scrambled to ask a different question from the one that had been decided on.

"Why not?"

"For reasons best known to herself, my sister has a burning desire to be ... a *doctor*."

There was a stunned silence. The film crew looked to the producer, but he nodded to them to keep the cameras rolling.

Pop didn't disappoint him.

"I'm where I want to be," she said, resting her hands on her heart. "All I wanted was to be famous. I love performing, and Rockley Park is wonderful for someone like me. But," she continued, "Lolly is different. We look identical, and we used to think the same way, too, but we don't anymore. I guess I want to make people happy." She turned to look at Lolly, and Lolly could see a tear welling up in the corner of her sister's eye. It sparkled in the bright lights like a precious jewel. "But Lolly wants to make people *well*." She took a deep breath, just controlling the wobble in her voice. "I'm so proud of her." Then her voice gave way, and the tear spilled in slow motion down her beautiful cheek.

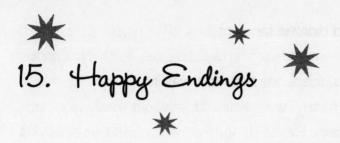

15. Happy Endings

Pop and Lolly were both in tears, their designer suits crushed in the huge hug they were giving each other. For all they cared, the room could have been completely empty. But, of course, it wasn't.

"When you caught my eye," sobbed Pop, "I suddenly realized. I wouldn't do anything I didn't want for two *seconds.* You've been trying to be kind...and I've been horrible."

The number two cameraman left his camera running on its stand. The number one cameraman walked backward a little so the girls would feel more private, but kept the close shot going by zooming the lens right in to focus on their faces. The soundman looked around for directions. The producer gestured for him to stay as he was, so the fluffy microphone stayed, suspended above the twins' heads.

Richard was ecstatic. This would make wonderful television. He totally ignored Satin, who was waving urgently at him from the other side of the room.

Eventually, Pop and Lolly disentangled themselves. Their makeup was ruined beyond repair, and tears were still shining in both their eyes. They looked at each other and Pop sighed.

"I'm so sorry."

"Me too."

"We'll figure something out."

"Of course we will." Lolly tried a smile.

Pop let out a small hiccup. "You look terrible."

"So do you," countered Lolly. Then she remembered where they were. "The cameras!"

Pop reached out and pushed a loose strand of hair behind her sister's ear. "Don't worry," she said, amazingly calm for a change. "It's not live. And Satin has a veto on any parts she doesn't like in the final edit.

You can stop now," she added sharply to the number one cameraman, who was moving in again.

Richard nodded, and the filming ceased.

As soon as the film crew started coiling up cables and dismantling the lights, Satin made a beeline for the twins.

"What was all that about you wanting to be a doctor?" she asked Lolly.

Pop and Lolly exchanged glances.

"It's a long story," said Lolly.

"You're young," Satin reminded them both. "There's lots of time to decide what you want to do with your lives." She gave Pop a long, hard look.

"That was a virtuoso performance, Pop, but I don't think you need to be quite so concerned about your sister rushing off to medical school just yet."

"It was my fault," Lolly said. "I got scared at the thought of having to work in the music industry for the rest of my life."

Satin sat down between the twins and put her arms around them both.

"I'm your agent, not your wicked stepmother," she said. "No agent worth their salt is going to force you to do something you don't want to do."

"But Pop *does* want to be a pop singer, and I don't," Lolly said, sniffing back her tears. "That's awful for her *and* for me."

"Nothing is forever," Satin said. "Believe me! Have you stopped enjoying the vacation modeling jobs I get you?"

"No, but ..."

"Have you stopped enjoying this school?"

"It's fun here," Lolly admitted.

"Well, then," said Satin. "You've already earned more than enough from modeling to put yourself through medical school without needing any sort of student loan. Why not relax and enjoy life? There's plenty of time to think about what you want to do for a career when you're older."

Lolly nodded. "I s'pose," she admitted. "But what about Pop?"

Satin laughed. "Judging by her skill in front of the camera, I'll bet Pop will be able to make a career out of singing, modeling, drama, talk-show hosting …you name it. The list is almost endless. She's a natural."

Pop hugged Satin. "And will you still be my agent, even if Pop 'n' Lolly doesn't exist anymore?"

"Of course I will. But my advice to you both is to keep on going the way you are as long as you both enjoy it. Do talk to your teachers about what you think you want to do, though, Lolly. They'll reassure you. I know someone from here who went on to become a lawyer. The help will be here if you want to go the academic route."

"So," said Pop to Lolly. "Are you going to stay at Rockley Park with me for a while longer?"

Lolly thought about it. "Are you going to stop teasing me about enjoying my science classes?" she said. They looked at each other, and then they both grinned.

"Hurrah!" yelled Marmalade, who was shamelessly eavesdropping.

Mr. Penardos clapped his hands. "Okay, everyone," he said to the class. "Let's get cleaned up. Tara, can you put tha' amp back in the corner? The staging can go against tha' wall. I have a class first thing in the morning, you know, so i' has to be done now."

Everyone worked with a will, and soon the wooden staging blocks that had been used to create the catwalk were all stacked neatly out of the way.

"I'm glad everything turned out okay," Chloe said to the twins. The three of them stood for a moment in a tight circle, hugging one another.

"You too," Pop told Tara, holding one arm out. "We four roommates are in this together, for better or for worse." Tara hesitated, and then allowed herself to be drawn into the circle.

"Actually," said Lolly, pulling back a little from the others. "I have another ambition."

Pop, Chloe, and Tara looked at her with worried faces.

"It's all right," she said with a smile, gathering them back into the huddle. "I'm not going to leave Rockley Park. And *whatever* we end up doing, I want us to stay friends like this forever!"

✳ ✳ So you want
to be a pop star?
✳
Turn the page to read some top tips
on how to make your dreams
✳ come true.... ✳
✳

✳ Making it in the music biz ✳

Think you've got tons of talent?
Well, music maestro Judge Jim Henson,
Head of Rock at top talent academy Rockley
Park, has put together his hot tips to help
you become a superstar…

✳ Number One Rule: Be positive!
You've got to believe in yourself.

✳ Be active! Join your school choir
or form your own band.

✳ Be different! Don't be afraid to stand
out from the crowd.

✳ Be determined! Work hard and stay focused.

✳ Be creative! Try writing your own material—
it will say something unique about you.

✳ Be patient! Don't give up if things
don't happen overnight.

✳ Be ready to seize opportunities
when they come along.

* Be versatile! Don't have a one-track mind—try out new things and gain as many skills as you can.

* Be passionate! Don't be afraid to show some emotion in your performance.

* Be sure to watch, listen, and learn all the time.

* Be willing to help others. You'll learn more that way.

* Be smart! Don't neglect your schoolwork.

* Be cool and don't get bigheaded! Everyone needs friends, so don't leave them behind.

* Always stay true to yourself.

* And finally, and most important, enjoy what you do!

*Go for it! It's all up to you now....

**For more about the
Fame School kids, read**

Danny's a truly talented drummer, and everyone at Rockley Park seems to know it. His friends, Chloe, Pop 'n' Lolly, Marmalade, and even rough-around-the-edges Tara are totally encouraging. But Charlie, the other drummer in seventh grade, is jealous of Danny's success. All Danny really wants to do is play the drums, but Charlie keeps getting in the way. When tension mounts between the two rivals, they're given a difficult punishment—they have to play a drumming duet in the school concert! The rivals have everything to play for, and everything to prove, but it seems that only one of them can come out on top. . . .

CINDY JEFFERIES's varied career has included being a Venetian-mask maker and a video DJ. Cindy decided to write *Fame School* after experiencing the ups and downs of her children, who have all been involved in the music business. Her insight into the lives of wannabe pop stars and her own musical background means that Cindy knows how exciting and demanding the quest for fame and fortune can be.

Cindy lives on a farm in Gloucestershire, England, where the animal noises, roaring tractors, and rehearsals of Stitch, her son's indie-rock band, all help her write!

To find out more about Cindy Jefferies, visit her Web site: www.cindyjefferies.co.uk